PARTY GIRLS

Caz's Birthday Blues

*Also in the **Party Girls** series*

PARTY GIRLS

Caz's Birthday Blues

Jennie Walters

illustrated by Jessie Eckel

Hodder
Children's
Books

a division of Hodder Headline Limited

For Holly, who had the original moon and stars party

First published in Great Britain in 2001
by Hodder Children's Books

10 9 8 7 6 5

ISBN 0 340 79586 7

Typeset by Hewer Text Ltd, Edinburgh
Printed and bound in Great Britain
by Bookmarque Ltd

Hodder Children's Books
a division of Hodder Headline Ltd
338 Euston Road
London NW1 3BH

FACT FILE: CAZ

Full name: Caroline Marie
  Bennett
Nicknames: Carrie, Caz
Family: mum Jackie,
  stepdad Michael, stepsister
  Natalie
Star sign: Taurus
Hair: blonde
Eyes: blue
Likes: shopping, reading, eating chocolate,
  phoning friends, writing my diary

Dislikes: school dinners,
  tidying my room, feeling left out,
  cabbage
Favourite food: Chinese
Favourite pizza topping: pepperoni
  and sweetcorn
Favourite thing in your
  wardrobe: black cropped trousers
Worst habit: biting my nails
Best quality: thinking
  about other people

NO-BITE
stop nail
biting now!

'So? What do you think?' Lauren said, peering down at the girl who'd just come into the garden of the house next door. 'She looks all right, doesn't she?'

'I love those trousers!' Michelle commented, craning over Lauren's shoulder for a closer look. 'Wonder where she got them from?'

'She's pretty, but I don't think she's going to be fun to hang around with,' Jess decided, tucking a stray lock of auburn hair behind one ear. 'She looks too cool to be much of a laugh.'

The three of them were in Lauren's bedroom, inspecting the new girl who'd just moved in next door. They'd been waiting ages to see if she would come out into the garden and now, here she was – sitting on a plastic chair and scuffing up the dirt with her shoe.

'Come on!' Lauren said with a grin, pushing Jess off the wide window seat. 'How can you possibly tell that? You haven't even spoken to her yet!'

'You don't need to speak to someone to know what they're like – trust me,' Jess said confidently, kneeling back up. 'I can read the signs.' She watched as the girl started wandering down the path towards a large brick shed in the middle of a wilderness at the bottom of the garden. 'And she's going to our school, right?' she asked.

'That's what Mum says,' Lauren answered. 'She went round there yesterday with a home-made cake. You know – trying to be a good neighbour and seeing what she could find out at the same time.'

'So, what's the story?' Michelle asked, turning away from the window at last. 'Has she got any brothers or sisters?'

'Oh yes?' Jess said, raising her eyebrows with a

knowing smile. 'Looking for a new crush are you, Miche?'

'Oh, give it a break!' Michelle exclaimed, blushing despite herself. 'For the last time, I do *not* have a thing about your creepy twin brother – got it?' She lunged forward suddenly, her long hair swinging, and pulled the hood of Jess's stripy top right over her head while she tickled her at the same time. Muffled shrieks of laughter came out from under the hood.

Lauren ignored them. 'Well, there's an older girl from the dad's first marriage,' she said. 'She's at sixth form college, Mum said. But Caroline – that's her name – is the same age as us, more or less, so she'll be in our year.'

'You'd better hope she's OK, then,' Jess muttered darkly, emerging from the hood. 'Imagine being stuck next door to Melissa Wilkins!'

The other two groaned. Melissa had made all their lives a misery at one time or another. She was always making catty remarks about what the other girls at school looked like, or how they played games, or where they lived and how much money their parents had. She usually went around in a gang with a couple of other girls – Lisa Watts and Ashley Taylor – but Lisa had moved away over the summer.

'Imagine if you had Melissa on one side of you and Ashley on the other!' Lauren said, and the thought was so terrible they stopped groaning and started to giggle.

'With Lisa in the house opposite,' Jess put in, and that made them all fall about. Michelle put her fingers down her throat and pretended to throw up, which brought on a major coughing fit and made Lauren and Jess laugh even harder.

'Hey, get down!' Jess suddenly gasped. 'She's looking at us!' And she dived to the ground, grabbing the nearest arm on her way – which happened to be Lauren's – and pulling her down too. Lauren collided with Michelle, and they all ended up in a sprawling heap on the floor.

Down in the garden, Caz gazed up at the house next door. There was that girl again – the one with the dark curly hair she'd caught a glimpse

4

of yesterday – and she had two friends with her. One was tall, and the other had auburn hair flopping over her face. The three of them had been watching her, Caz could tell, and now they were all making sick noises and laughing.

Caz felt her cheeks begin to burn and glanced away quickly, jamming her fists into the pockets of her combats as she walked back towards the house. She did her best not to look like she was hurrying, but she couldn't wait to get inside, away from those staring eyes. How would *they* like it, she thought fiercely to herself, moving to a horrible house with poky little rooms that hadn't been decorated in the last hundred years? And having to start all over again at a new school where they didn't know anyone? They wouldn't think life was so funny *then*, would they?

She kicked open the back door and stomped into the kitchen, where her mother was kneeling on the floor unpacking crockery. Piles of scrumpled newspaper lay everywhere, and the table was covered in towering stacks of plates and bowls. Caz caught a saucepan with her foot and sent it spinning across the lino.

'What's the matter with you?' her mother said mildly, leaning forward to field the pan.

'I'm bored,' Caz answered grumpily, slumping down on a chair that was standing adrift in the middle of the room. 'There's nothing to do here.'

'There's lots to do!' her mother protested, holding a glass up to the light and looking at the rim to see if it was chipped. 'You could start putting away all your clothes, for a start. There won't be much time once school's started.'

'Might as well leave them in the boxes,' Caz answered gloomily, getting to her feet. 'I haven't got anywhere to hang them, have I?'

The removal men hadn't been able to fit her wardrobe round the narrow, curved landing. It had ended up in her stepsister's room at the top of the stairs.

'Oh come on, Carrie,' her mother sighed, sitting back on her heels. 'Couldn't you *try* to be a bit more positive? It isn't easy for any of us, moving to a smaller house, but we've all got to make an effort. Cheer up, love! After all, it's your birthday in a couple of weeks.'

'Great,' Caz muttered, on her way out of the room. The way she was feeling at the moment, her birthday was only something else to worry about. How could she have a party with no friends? Besides, her bedroom was too small for a sleepover. At this rate, she'd end up watching videos all evening and feeling sorry for herself. And her birthday fell on a Saturday this year. What a waste!

Thumping up the stairs, giving each one a really good stamp with her trainers, Caz went into her room and lay down on the bed. She felt a twinge of guilt, knowing her mother was only trying to help, but she'd sunk too deeply into a bad mood to snap out of it now. She stared gloomily round her new bedroom. It was full of boxes, stacked one on top of the other and bursting with clothes, shoes and books. Her old room must have been three times the size of this one. How was she ever going to fit everything in?

With a sigh, Caz turned over on to her tummy and reached under the pillow for her diary.

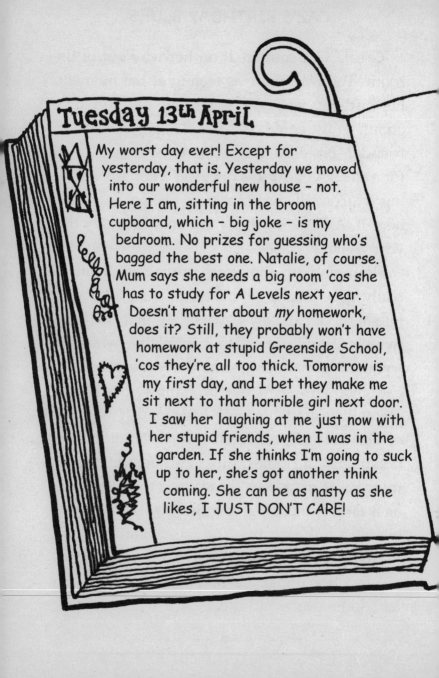

Tuesday 13th April

My worst day ever! Except for yesterday, that is. Yesterday we moved into our wonderful new house – not. Here I am, sitting in the broom cupboard, which – big joke – is my bedroom. No prizes for guessing who's bagged the best one. Natalie, of course. Mum says she needs a big room 'cos she has to study for A Levels next year. Doesn't matter about *my* homework, does it? Still, they probably won't have homework at stupid Greenside School, 'cos they're all too thick. Tomorrow is my first day, and I bet they make me sit next to that horrible girl next door. I saw her laughing at me just now with her stupid friends, when I was in the garden. If she thinks I'm going to suck up to her, she's got another think coming. She can be as nasty as she likes, I JUST DON'T CARE!

'Hey, you lot!' Lauren's mother called up the stairs next door. 'You've got a visitor. Sunny's back!'

'Sunny!' screamed Lauren, Michelle and Jess together, rushing out on to the landing. Sunny was already halfway up the stairs, grinning fit to burst, her glossy black hair streaming out behind her.

'Did you miss me?' she asked, as the three of them crowded round her. 'Has it been boring round here while I've been away?'

'Seems like you've been gone for *ever*,' Michelle said, linking arms with Sunny and dragging her into Lauren's room.

'Oh, come on!' Jess chipped in. 'At least we've had some peace and quiet for a while.'

'So tell us all about it,' Lauren said, as the four of them flopped down on the bed with Sunny in the middle. 'Did you have a great time in India? Should we be really jealous?'

'It was fantastic,' Sunny said, leaning back on the bed with a faraway look in her eyes. 'Fan-tas-tic! We started off in Delhi so my dad could do some business – that was a bit boring – but then we went to Bombay to stay with my aunties and uncles, and that was the best ever! I went round all the time with my cousin Meera and she showed me the best places to shop. The markets are great – really cheap! I brought back a load of clothes.'

'This is beautiful,' Lauren said, fingering the sleeve of Sunny's thin purple cotton top. 'I love those beads round the hem.'

'Wait till you see what I've got you,' Sunny said, digging into the big embroidered bag over her shoulder. There was a beaded purse for Jess (orange, to match her hair), a red cotton tunic for Lauren (to make her look even more of a hippy), and a pair of satin slippers for Michelle (to go with all the trendy skirts she liked wearing).

'No heels, see?' Sunny said, craning forward to look as Michelle tried the sandals on.

Michelle was the tallest in her class, though she hated people going on about it. She threw Sunny a warning look, but Sunny only grinned and said, 'You'll be a model one of these days, I know it. Go on, give us a twirl!'

So Michelle flicked her hair back, smoothed down her faded denim skirt and started walking down the room with very precise steps, putting one foot exactly in front of the other. The others all burst out laughing.

'What's that expression on your face?' Jess shrieked. 'Are you going to be sick or something?'

'It's what all the models do,' Michelle protested. 'I've seen them on TV! You've got to pretend there's a bad smell under your nose. It makes you look cool.'

'Makes you look stupid, more like,' Jess snorted.

'Where's Nikki? Isn't she coming over?' Sunny asked, taking the last present out of her bag.

'She should be here any minute,' Lauren said,

looking up at the Snoopy clock on her bedroom wall. 'Her dad's dropping her round after swimming. Did Mum tell you she's taking us all bowling? One last treat to make up for school starting tomorrow.'

'Great,' Sunny said, settling back on the bed and making herself comfortable. 'Well, come on, then – tell me all the gossip. What's been going on?'

'The new family's moved in next door at last,' Lauren said, sitting cross-legged on the floor and hugging her knees. 'There's a girl our age called Caroline and, guess what – she's going to our school!'

'We were watching her in the garden just now, but she looked up and saw us,' Jess said. She got up and went back over to the window. 'Let's wait and see if she comes out again.'

'You lot are *so* sad!' Sunny exclaimed. 'Why don't we just go round and say hello?'

'Maybe we could ask her to come bowling with us,' Jess suggested, turning her back to the view and sitting down on the windowsill with a thump.

'We don't know what she's like, though,' Michelle objected, taking off the sandals and pushing her feet back into her shoes. 'She might be horrible, and then we'd be stuck with her.'

'No, I think it's a good idea,' Lauren said. 'I felt bad when she caught us all staring and we just fell about – we should have waved or something. Let's invite her out with us. There'd be room for one more in the car if we squash up, and Mum won't mind taking Caroline as well. She's been on at me to meet her, anyway.'

Before the others could say any more, the bedroom door was flung open and a girl with wavy blonde hair came bursting in. She was wearing black Adidas trackies with poppers up the side and a white Ellesse shirt that brought out her tan. 'Hey, Sunny!' she grinned, giving her a high five. 'I'd nearly forgotten what you looked like.'

'Sunny's brought us all pressies,' Jess said. 'Look at my purse – isn't it cool?'

'Great,' Nikki said, expertly catching the last package Sunny had tossed her. She ripped open the paper and out fell a baseball cap with 'Bom-

13

bay Tigers' in swirly letters across the front. 'Wow – thanks!' she said, jamming it on over her damp hair. 'This'll be perfect for tennis.'

'Come on, you lot!' Lauren's mum Valerie called up. 'You're going to miss your slot at the bowling alley if we don't get a move on.'

'Mum, can we see if the girl next door wants to come with us?' Lauren asked as they all piled down the stairs.

'That's a good idea,' her mother said absent-mindedly, searching through her bag. 'Why don't you go and ask her while I get the car out? If I can ever find my keys, that is.'

'Go on, then,' Michelle said to Lauren as they stood on the doorstep of the house next door. 'If you think this is such a good idea, why don't you ring the bell?'

'Stop rushing me!' Lauren replied. Her hand

hovered over the doorbell, but then she stuck it back in the pocket of her jeans and turned round to Nikki and Jess, who were just behind her. 'What do you think?' she asked them. 'Maybe we should just keep it to the five of us, after all?'

Jess shrugged her shoulders. 'Might as well be friendly,' she said.

'Yeah,' Nikki added. 'And even if we don't like her, a couple of hours' bowling won't kill us, will it?'

'I think we should forget about it,' Michelle said. 'We'll meet her tomorrow at school. And if she saw Jess's performance, she probably thinks we're all idiots anyway.'

'Oh, thanks very much!' Jess said indignantly.

'Then this is our chance to show her we're not,' Sunny said, pushing forward and ringing the doorbell. 'Come on, she won't bite.'

The five of them stood there on the doorstep, listening to the tinny chime of the doorbell fade away somewhere inside the house, and wondering who would come to answer it.

'This door could do with a coat of paint,' Michelle whispered, gazing at the peeling wood.

'So could the whole house,' Lauren told her. 'Mrs Jones hadn't done anything to it for years. You should see the – oh, um, hello!'

The door had swung open, and a tired-looking woman in jeans with a scarf over her hair was standing in front of them.

'I'm Lauren, from next door,' Lauren said awkwardly, blushing. 'We were going bowling – me and my friends – and we wondered if your daughter would like to come.'

'Oh, that's nice of you,' said the woman, breaking into a beaming smile which made them all feel more comfortable. 'I'm Jackie – Caroline's mum. Come on in for a second and you can ask her yourselves.'

The girls filed in and stood in the narrow hallway, while Jackie shouted up the stairs. 'Caroline! Carrie! Come down – there are visitors for you.'

'Why can't you call me Caz, like everyone else?' came the grumpy reply, floating down through an open bedroom door. Sunny raised her eyebrows and nudged Michelle, who smiled. Jess frowned at them.

'OK! So this is Caz,' said her mother brightly, as Caz came down the stairs. 'Well, I'd better get back to the unpacking and leave you to introduce yourselves.'

'I'm Lauren,' Lauren said, wondering why it was so difficult to say your own name. 'I live next door.'

'I know,' said Caz, tucking her blonde hair behind one ear. 'I've seen you a couple of times.'

'We were just going bowling,' Lauren went on. 'Do you want to come? Oh, these are my friends, by the way – Sunny, Michelle, Jess and Nikki.'

Caz threw them a quick look, not really taking in the list of names Lauren was rattling off. Yes, there was the tall girl, and the redhead – she hadn't seen the other two before. So they'd all come round to check her out, had they? Well, she wasn't going to let them see how awkward that made her feel.

'Sorry – I'm a bit busy at the moment,' she said in an offhand voice. 'I'm trying to get everything sorted out before tomorrow.'

'You're starting at Greenside, aren't you?' Sunny broke in. 'That's where we all go.'

'Have you got your sweatshirt yet?' Jess asked. 'Gross, isn't it?'

'Yeah, it certainly is,' Caz said, smiling for the first time. For a second, she wondered if she'd been too quick to turn down their invitation. They all seemed quite friendly, now that she'd had a proper look at them. Maybe they hadn't been laughing at her in the garden after all. And it would have been fun to go bowling. Still – too late now.

There was an awkward silence for a few seconds. 'Thanks for asking me, anyway,' Caz said eventually. 'I s'pose I'll see you tomorrow at school.'

'Well, you can't say we didn't try,' said Jess, as they piled into the car which Lauren's mum had reversed out into the street. 'Not very friendly, is she?'

'Give her time,' Valerie advised, starting the engine again. 'She's probably just feeling shy. After all, there are five of you and only one of her.'

'She looks a bit snobby to me,' Michelle said, reaching for her safety belt. 'And she was really rude to her mum. Did you hear her?'

'Oh, like you never talk back to yours, I suppose,' Lauren said. It was all right for Michelle and Jess – they lived a couple of doors away from each other and were never stuck for company. She'd have loved to have a friend next door.

By the time they'd arrived at the bowling alley,

though, she was feeling more cheerful. After all, it was the last day of the Easter holidays – they might as well enjoy themselves.

The place was packed out. 'Just as well we booked,' Lauren's mum said as they stood in the queue. 'Looks like everyone else has had the same idea.'

To make matters worse, there was a young trainee on the front desk. 'I'll take over here, Pete,' the manager said eventually, coming over when he saw how many people were waiting. 'You can give out the shoes.'

At last, Valerie had paid. 'Lane twenty-three,' the manager said, slapping a ticket down on the counter, so they went over to change into rubber-soled shoes.

'I'll catch you later,' Lauren's mum said to the girls, making for the café. 'Think I'll sit and read my paper while you guys play.'

Pete was getting more flustered by the minute. The bowling shoes were numbered, and each pair was stored in a pigeon hole with that same number. He kept putting the customers' shoes back into the wrong pigeon holes. On top of that, everyone seemed to want the same size.

'Another size three?' he said to Lauren as she laid her trainers on the counter. 'I think we've run out.'

'I can see a pair down there,' Lauren pointed out. 'Look, in the bottom corner.'

Pete went off to investigate.

'Well, aren't those smart?' said a silky voice in Lauren's ear. She whirled around to see none other than Melissa Wilkins, the class bully herself, staring at her trainers. Melissa was wearing a short black jacket with the collar turned up, and her long brown hair was scraped into a topknot with a white scrunchie. 'New, are they?' she went on, picking up the shoes and turning them over in her hands.

'My auntie sent them over from the States,' Lauren replied, wanting to snatch the trainers out of Melissa's hands. They'd only arrived a few days ago, and they were her pride and joy. She didn't want Melissa touching them – or Ashley, who was hovering at her shoulder as usual, trying to see what was going on.

'Very nice,' Melissa said, with a glint in her eye. Pete came back with a pair of bowling shoes in his hands, so Melissa gave him the trainers and took the shoes in return.

'What are you doing?' Lauren asked, alarmed. 'Those bowling shoes are for me!'

'Keep your hair on,' Melissa said sweetly, chucking them over. 'Just being helpful. Ashley and me have finished anyway – we've come to get our own shoes back.'

Lauren felt as though Melissa's eyes were boring into her back as she walked over to the bowling lane with her friends. Still, at least she and Ashley were leaving, not hanging round to sneer. She risked a quick look back at the shoe counter to see if they'd gone, and her eyes suddenly widened in disbelief. It couldn't be, could it? Surely not! And yet—

Melissa had handed in her bowling shoes, and was being passed a pair of trainers over the counter. Smart new trainers. *Lauren's* trainers.

'Stop!' she cried desperately, starting to run while Jess and the others stared after her in surprise. 'Those are mine! Put them down!'

By the time she'd got to the counter, Melissa had put the trainers on and was calmly tying up the laces. 'What are you doing with my shoes?' Lauren demanded, skidding to a halt and trying to catch her breath. She clutched the inhaler in her pocket, making an effort to calm down in case she was heading for an asthma attack. She hadn't had one for ages – her new breathing exercises were really helping – but she hadn't been so stressed for ages, either.

'*Your* shoes?' Melissa replied coolly, looking up at her. 'Don't know what you're talking about. These are mine.'

'No, they're not!' Lauren shouted, tears of anger and frustration prickling at her eyes. 'How can you say that? You know they're mine! Give them back!'

'Give them back! Give them back!' Melissa mimicked in a baby voice. Then she hissed spitefully, 'I'm not giving them back because they're *mine*. They are now, anyway. Got that?'

23

'Got that?' Ashley repeated, giving Lauren a shove. 'They're Melissa's, not yours. You crazy or something?'

'What's going on?' said Jess, who'd come over to see what all the fuss was about.

'She's got my trainers,' Lauren said, pointing at Melissa's feet. 'Look!'

Jess stared at Melissa as though she couldn't quite believe her eyes. Melissa stared defiantly back, crossing her arms over her chest. Jess began to flush red with anger. Then she leaned across the counter and said to Pete in a loud voice, 'Excuse me! There's been a mix-up here. You've given someone back the wrong shoes.'

At first he pretended not to hear, but Jess

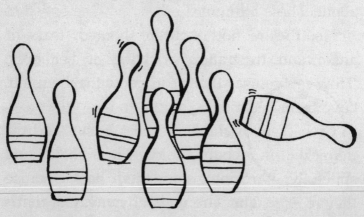

wasn't prepared to give up – she kept on calling. Melissa tried to leave, but by now Nikki, Sunny and Michelle were standing there too, blocking her path.

Eventually Pete came over. 'What's the problem?' he asked reluctantly.

Lauren showed him the number on her bowling shoes, and he checked the corresponding pigeon hole where her trainers should have been. It was empty. Then he managed to remember which bowling shoes Melissa had just returned, and looked at the number on them.

'These must be hers,' he said sheepishly, taking a grubby pair of shoes from the next-door pigeon hole. 'Sorry – I didn't look at the number. She told me those trainers belonged to her, so I didn't bother to check.'

Everyone turned to stare at Melissa. Without a word, she kicked the trainers off, not bothering to undo the laces, and snatched her shoes off the counter. Michelle, Nikki and Sunny stood aside to let her go and she walked quickly towards the exit, Ashley following on behind. As they reached the door, she turned round and shot Lauren a look of pure hatred.

Lauren hugged her trainers tightly as the door swung shut behind the pair of them. 'Thanks, Jess,' she said. 'You were great!'

'That's OK,' Jess said, linking an arm through Lauren's. 'She thinks she can get away with anything, that girl! She just needs standing up to. You're too sweet, Lauren – that's your problem.'

'Not like the Red Devil here,' Sunny said, tweaking Jess's hair. 'I reckon even Ashley's scared of you, Jess.'

'Well, they've gone now,' Michelle said, prising the precious trainers out of Lauren's grip. 'Give these back and let's get on with the game. We've got to stop Nikki winning for once, remember?'

'Huh! You don't stand a chance,' Nikki said, punching the air.

As they walked over to the bowling lane, chatting and laughing, the butterflies in Lauren's stomach gradually subsided. She knew she could rely on her friends. What could Melissa do to hurt her?

'Now, before I take the register, I'd like you all to meet the new girl who's joining us this term,' Mrs Ryder said, smiling encouragingly at the class. She had wiry grey hair and an anxious expression.

'This is Caroline Bennett, everyone,' she went on, and Caz felt what seemed like a hundred pairs of eyes swivelling in her direction. Lauren's were among them, and Caz also recognised the tall girl she'd met the day before, though she'd forgotten her name. She gave a vague, all-purpose smile round the room, before looking back down at the carpet as quickly as she could.

Greenside was so weird! At her last school, they'd sat facing the blackboard in rows. Here, they sat in little groups around tables that had been pushed together. Caz wasn't used to having boys in the classroom either. She happened to notice that the boy next to her was playing on a Game Boy which he'd hidden in his lap. So did Mrs Ryder.

'I'll take that, thank you, Jamie,' she said sharply, swooping down on him and snatching the Game Boy out of his hands. 'You can have it back at the end of school, but if I see it again, I'll confiscate it till the end of term. Understand?'

'Yes, Miss,' Jamie replied, pulling a face.

'Good,' Mrs Ryder snapped. Then she put on her bright, encouraging voice again and said to the girl on the other side of Caz, 'Now, Becky, would you like to be Caroline's special friend and show her where everything is for the first couple of days?'

'Yes, please, Mrs Ryder,' Becky replied eagerly, shuffling even closer to Caz and giving her a toothy grin. She was a tall, thin girl with short brown hair that stood up in spikes like a hedgehog's. 'And Mrs Ryder, I've read all those books you recommended. Do you want reviews of my top ten for the school magazine?'

'Come and see me at break,' Mrs Ryder said, blinking worriedly. 'Well done! You've obviously been working very hard.'

Caz guessed that Becky must be the class boff. Teachers usually picked somebody like that to show the new girl round. She smiled to herself, and caught Lauren's eye at the opposite table. Lauren smiled back, as though she knew just what Caz was thinking, and winked at her. Caz immediately felt a hundred times better. Lauren looked so nice, with that cloud of curly hair and her big brown eyes, and she didn't seem to hold any hard feelings from the day before. Caz decided to try and make friends with her at break.

There were assembly and a couple of lessons to get through before then, though. Becky was taking her job as helper very seriously. She watched Caz like a hawk most of the time, which made her feel nervous and inclined to drop things.

'Here – borrow mine,' Becky whispered, when Caz's pencil had rolled on to the floor for the third time in their English lesson.

'Thanks,' Caz whispered back, gingerly taking the pencil Becky offered her. It was all wet and chewed at the end, so she tried to wipe it on her skirt without Becky noticing. She didn't want to hurt her feelings.

When the bell rang for break, Becky zoomed in on Caz immediately. 'I usually go to the library at break,' she said. 'Or I could show you the playground, if you'd like that better?'

'Let's start off in the playground,' Caz suggested. If she was shut away with Becky in the library, she'd never get a chance to meet up with Lauren and the others. 'I've got some crisps we could share.'

'Great!' Becky replied, her eyes shining. 'My mum won't let me have crisps because of all the additives.'

She took Caz out to the playground at the back of the classrooms, with Portakabins along one side of it. They stood with their backs to the wall, eating crisps and watching everyone else doing their usual break-time things. Some of the boys played footie with a tennis ball, and lots of the younger girls were skipping or rushing about chasing each other. Caz could see Lauren chatting to her friends, but she felt she couldn't just abandon Becky to join them.

Then she became aware that two people were walking up. She'd noticed one of them in her class – a small girl with a thin face and long brown hair in a plait. Her friend was taller and heavier, with wavy blonde hair and a square jaw.

'Clear off, creep,' the smaller girl said to Becky in a matter-of-fact voice, while the big blonde girl at her shoulder glared menacingly.

'OK,' Becky replied, sounding not the least bit surprised. She licked the cheese-and-onion crumbs off her fingers and added, 'Thanks for the crisps, Caz. I'll see you after break,' before scooting off.

The first girl looked Caz up and down, from the top of her untidy ponytail to the tip of her nerdy new school shoes. Caz looked back, knowing that she was being measured up for coolness but trying to show that she didn't care.

'My name's Melissa,' the girl said eventually, smiling with her mouth but not her eyes. 'I'm in your class. And this is my mate, Ashley.'

The blonde girl behind her leaned forward to peer at the crisp packet Caz was holding. 'Got any of those left?' she asked hopefully.

'No, sorry,' Caz answered, showing her the empty bag. 'You're just too late.'

'We thought we'd come and rescue you,' Melissa said with a sneer. 'You don't want to be stuck with Becky all day.'

'She's all right,' Caz replied stoutly, feeling guilty that she'd had exactly the same thought herself a few minutes ago.

'She's a creep, all right,' Melissa snorted, and Ashley sniggered as if the joke was the funniest thing she'd heard. 'You can come and sit with us on the bench,' Melissa went on, making it sound like a big privilege. 'We'll tell you who's worth bothering with in this school.'

She took Caz's arm in a steely grip and steered her over to the only seat in the playground. Some third years who'd been playing tag around it scattered like a shoal of startled fish as the three of them approached.

Caz would rather have been holed up in the library with Becky than stuck on the bench with Melissa and Ashley. There wasn't much she could do about it, though, except sit tight and see what they were after.

In a couple of minutes, Melissa managed to worm all sorts of things out of Caz that she'd rather not have told her, including the fact that she'd been a boarder at her last school.

'Your parents must have loads of money,' Melissa said, narrowing her eyes. 'I should think Greenside's a bit of a comedown, after a posh place like that.'

'Not really,' Caz said, shrugging her shoulders. In fact, leaving boarding school had been a big relief. She didn't like being away from her mum and most of the other girls had been major show-offs. They were always boasting about who had the trendiest clothes, or whose parents had the biggest car.

There was a pause. Ashley chewed gum. Melissa examined her plait for split ends. Caz bit her nails.

'Did you go anywhere good for Easter?' Melissa asked eventually.

'Nah,' Ashley replied, swapping gum from one cheek to the other.

'Not you, stupid!' Melissa snapped. 'I know *you* hung around the shopping centre for two weeks. I was talking to *her*.' And she jerked her head at Caz.

'Don't have a nervous breakdown,' Ashley muttered, flushing red.

Caz knew that Melissa wasn't worth trying to impress. All the same, she didn't particularly want her to know that the Bennett/Brown family hadn't gone away either. Things had been very difficult at home since her stepdad had lost his job in the new year. Even moving to a smaller house – 'downsizing' as her mother called it – hadn't left any spare money over for holidays.

'We went to Italy,' she said airily, remembering a travel programme she'd seen on the TV a couple of days before. 'By the lakes. There's an amazing hotel we've stayed at a couple of times, right on the water.'

'Sounds great,' Melissa said, though there was

a suspicious gleam in her eye. 'What's it called, then, this hotel?'

'The Margharita,' Caz said, looking steadily back at her. It was the only Italian word she could think of.

'Like the pizza?' Ashley said, showing some interest for the first time.

'That's right,' Caz replied, thinking fast. 'It's a speciality of the hotel. People come from miles around to eat there.'

She tried to think of a way to change the subject – this whole Italian holiday thing could easily get out of hand. Standing up, she said casually, 'I'm just going to have a word with Lauren. Guess I'll see you later.'

'Lauren?' Melissa replied, the corners of her mouth drooping down into their usual sneer. 'How do you know *her*?'

'She lives next door to me,' Caz replied, surprised by the venom in Melissa's voice.

'Lucky you,' Melissa said sarcastically, as the bell rang to announce the end of break. 'Well, let me tell you something. If you want to be friends with us, you'd better steer clear of Lauren – and those sad losers she hangs round with.'

She got lazily to her feet and tugged down her short skirt before adding, 'And if you *are* friends with us, you'll probably enjoy Greenside a lot more than if you're not. Understand?'

Caz understood very well, and felt her stomach sinking. Melissa was giving her a clear warning. And, if she decided to ignore it, she could end up with a couple of powerful enemies on her hands . . .

'So, what do you think?' Michelle asked, putting her head round Lauren and Jess's cubicle in the changing rooms. She scooped up her long hair and twirled around so they had a good view of the electric blue T-shirt she was wearing. 'Is this better than the dress?'

'Hmm.' Lauren looked at her critically. 'The colour's great, but I don't like the way it's gathered at the top. Makes you look too skinny.'

'Maybe you're right,' Michelle said, pushing in front of Jess to have another gawp in the mirror. 'I might try that zip-up shirt again.'

'Miche!' Jess exclaimed, jumping up and down to try and get a look at her own reflection. 'Go back to your own cubicle! We're too crowded in here already!'

Lauren wasn't trying anything on, but she'd come in with Jess to keep her company. It was the middle of Saturday morning, peak shopping time, and all the changing rooms were packed out.

'I love these embroidered jeans,' Jess said, looking at herself in the mirror when Michelle had gone. 'I think I'll ask Mum if I can have them for my birthday.'

'It's not your birthday for ages.' Michelle's voice came floating over the partition from the next-door cubicle. 'A couple of months at least!'

'So?' Jess retorted. 'I might not see anything else I like before then.'

'Very likely – I don't think,' Lauren said, smiling.

They went to the shopping centre all the time. Michelle's mother was a beauty therapist in a big department store there and she often had to work on Saturdays, so Michelle would go round to Jess's house and spend the day with her. Jess's mum was happy to drop them both off at the centre for a couple of hours, with any of the other girls who wanted to come. Today, only Lauren could make it: Nikki was playing in a tennis tournament and Sunny was away visiting her auntie for the weekend.

'Come on, let's make a move,' Lauren said to Jess, looking at her watch. 'Are you going to buy anything, Miche?'

'Nope! Haven't got any money,' Michelle said, coming out of her cubicle with a huge armful of clothes. She dumped them on the reject rail, ignoring the glares of the shop assistant and the queue of people waiting for a free cubicle.

'Not so loud!' Lauren hissed. 'You don't have to shout about it!'

Giggling, they made their way out of the changing rooms and back on to the shop floor.

'Hey, there's your next-door neighbour,' Jess said, nudging Lauren's arm. 'Caz – that's her name, isn't it? And guess who's with her.'

'Melissa!' Lauren groaned, her heart sinking. 'Great! That's all we need.'

'What do you think of this?' Melissa asked Caz, pulling out a sparkly black T-shirt with gold lacing up the front. 'Nice, isn't it?'

'Yeah, great,' Caz said half-heartedly. She thought the top looked really tarty, though she didn't dare say so. She drifted over to a rail of leather jackets, wishing she and her mum hadn't bumped into Melissa at the entrance to the shopping centre, and that her mum hadn't suggested that the two of them went round the shops together.

Caz had got to know Melissa a little better over the past few days at school, but she still didn't like her very much. She was always poking fun at people, and she was really nasty to the younger kids and loners like Becky. Caz would much sooner have made friends with somebody else, but no one came near her when she was sitting on the bench with Melissa and Ashley.

Melissa appeared at her shoulder. 'Not going to get one of those, are you?' she asked, looking enviously at the jackets. 'They cost a fortune!'

'I wish!' Lauren said, looking at the price tag.

She was just about to add that it was her birthday in a week's time, and maybe her mum would be buying something nice for her, when she bit her tongue. Melissa would be bound to start asking whether she was going to have a party, and she couldn't think of anyone she'd want to invite. Certainly not Melissa and Ashley. She'd sooner spend the evening with her scary stepsister, Natalie!

'Well, look who it isn't,' Melissa said, looking over to the other side of the shop. 'Little Miss Perfect and her friends!'

Caz followed her gaze and saw Lauren with Michelle, and the red-haired girl in the other class whose name she could never remember. They were chatting and laughing together, as if they were having a great time. Caz felt a twinge of jealousy – here she was, stuck with catty Melissa.

'Thinks she's so wonderful,' Melissa sneered, staring at Lauren. 'Just look at her, with all that stupid curly hair!

'I really like her hair,' Caz objected quietly, but Melissa wasn't listening.

'I'm going to teach her a lesson,' she went on, turning to Caz and smiling unpleasantly. 'Just watch! This is going to be fun.'

She glanced quickly around to see if any of the shop assistants were watching. Then, in front of Caz's horrified eyes, she whipped a purple silk shirt off the hanger and stuffed it under her baggy sweatshirt.

'What are you doing?' Caz asked, appalled. 'Are you nicking that?'

'No, Lauren is – though she doesn't know it yet,' Melissa replied maliciously. 'I'm going to get that little goody goody into trouble for once in her life. Her dorky friends won't get her out of *this* one!'

Before Caz could stop her, Melissa sauntered over to Lauren and the others. Caz couldn't hear the conversation, but she saw the way Lauren stiffened as Melissa approached, and how the other two crowded round protectively behind her. She also saw Melissa secretly drop the shirt into an open carrier bag at Lauren's feet. There was a quick flash of purple as it slithered down into the bag, and Caz caught a glimpse of the cream plastic security tag too.

It was all over in a few seconds. 'Well?' Melissa crowed, grinning with delight as she joined Caz again. 'Did you see that? Easy! Now all we have to do is sit back and watch what happens when she goes out of the shop.' And she imitated the sound of a police siren.

'But she's going to get into so much trouble!' Caz protested, still hardly able to believe what Melissa had just done.

'I know!' Melissa replied delightedly. 'I can't wait!'

Caz watched, appalled, as Lauren walked towards the exit with her friends. She felt as though she was trapped in a nightmare, unable to speak or move. Then Lauren glanced quickly over in their direction, and Caz caught her eye. The spell was broken.

'Wait!' she shouted urgently, waving as she hurried over. She *had* to stop Lauren going out of the shop. Could she make it in time?

Lauren paused, one step away from the barrier. 'What's the matter?' she asked suspiciously. 'Got another charming message from Melissa?'

'Check your carrier bag,' Caz said quietly,

looking round to see if the security guard was anywhere near by. 'There's something in there you don't know about.'

Lauren opened the bag, and gasped when she realised what was inside. 'How did that get there?' she asked Caz in a startled voice.

'I'll give you three guesses,' Caz replied, and saw understanding begin to dawn on Lauren's face.

Jess took a quick look into the bag too, and then glanced around the shop. 'Careful! The security guard's looking at us!' she hissed urgently.

'What am I going to do?' Lauren asked, trying not to panic.

'Here, pass it over,' Caz said hurriedly. 'I'll put it back on the hanger.'

Jess came closer to shield Lauren as she fumbled in the carrier bag. Caz held her denim jacket open for a second and, in a flash, Lauren had tucked the shirt inside it.

'Thanks!' she whispered. 'I owe you one.'

Caz walked back though the shop, her hands damp with sweat and her heart pounding. What if someone had seen them? At last she made it back to the right rail, pulled the shirt out from under her jacket and slipped it back on the empty hanger. It was slightly creased, but that was all.

'Can I help you with anything?' A shop assistant had appeared out of nowhere, and was staring at her with eagle eyes.

'Just looking, thanks,' Caz stammered. 'Don't think you've got my size.' She flipped through the rest of the shirts on the rail with trembling hands, then walked away.

'What did you go and do that for?' All of a sudden Melissa was standing in front of her. She glared at Caz menacingly. 'Another goody two-shoes, are you?'

'I couldn't just stand there and let her be accused of stealing!' Caz protested. 'What have you got against Lauren, anyway? What's she ever done to you?'

'That's none of your business,' Melissa snapped. 'The only thing that matters is that *I* had a great idea and *you* ruined it.' She suddenly leant forward and grabbed Caz's arm, digging her nails into the soft skin so sharply that tears came to Caz's eyes. 'I won't forget that in a hurry,' she hissed, before turning on her heel and stalking out of the shop.

Caz watched her go through blurry eyes. Well, that's just wonderful, she thought to herself, rubbing her sore arm. Not only do I have no friends at school – but now I've managed to make one major enemy as well.

'Are you OK?'

Caz whirled around to find Jess standing next to her in the shop. She nodded, not quite trusting herself to speak.

'What's she done?' Jess asked, noticing that Caz was still cradling her arm. Her hazel eyes widened when Caz stretched it out with a rueful smile, and she saw the four deep red crescents that Melissa's fingernails had left behind. 'That girl is so mean!' she breathed. 'We can't let her get away with it.'

'She gets away with everything,' Caz said, rubbing her eyes with the back of her hand and suddenly feeling very sorry for herself.

'No, she doesn't,' Jess said firmly. 'You stood up against her just now, didn't you?' She looked

47

at Caz again and seemed to make up her mind about something. 'We're all going for lunch now,' she said. 'Can you come too? The café's just along from here.'

'But my mum's with me,' Caz said, taken by surprise and blurting out the first thing that came into her head, then feeling embarrassed.

'That's OK, so's mine,' Jess told her. 'And Lauren's. Your mum can have a mega gossip session with them, and we can work out what to do about the Poison Dwarf. Come on – I'm starving!'

'OK,' Caz said with a shaky smile. 'That would be great. Thanks!'

She followed Jess towards the exit, where Michelle and Lauren were waiting, and her spirits began to rise as they rushed up to talk to her. Maybe Melissa's nasty little plan had backfired.

'But we thought you were such good friends with Melissa and Ashley!' Lauren said when the four girls were sitting round a table in the café, a safe distance away from their mothers.

'No way!' Caz exclaimed. 'I don't know why

48

they always wanted me to sit with them. Melissa never seemed to like me very much in the first place.'

'She always takes control when someone new comes along,' Jess said, slurping up her fruit smoothie through a straw. 'It's like she's frightened to let them talk to anybody else. She's always ganging up on people and picking fights.'

'Besides, her best friend left last term,' Michelle added. 'She's probably looking for a replacement.'

Caz groaned, and the expression on her face made them all laugh.

'Melissa's the meanest girl in the whole year,' Lauren said. She spooned up some froth from the top of her strawberry milkshake. 'You were really brave to stand up to her like that. Thanks! I don't know what I'd have done if they'd found that shirt in my bag.'

'She hates me now, though,' Caz said miserably. 'I'm not looking forward to seeing her in school on Monday.'

'She hates everyone,' Jess said. 'Don't worry

about it – if it gets too bad, you can always tell Mrs Ryder. Loads of people have complained about Melissa. They'll suspend her if she carries on like this.'

At that moment, a harassed-looking waitress bustled up with their order.

'I wish we'd gone to Burger King,' Michelle grumbled, looking down at her toasted cheese-and-tomato sandwich.

'You eat chips all the time!' Lauren replied. 'I don't know why you aren't covered in spots and the size of a house. Besides, I'm sick of bean-burgers.'

'You still haven't eaten any meat?' Jess asked, wrinkling her freckled nose. 'Not even the teen-iest bacon roll? Ham sandwich? Hot dog?'

'No, nothing,' Lauren said. 'Not for three months, and I haven't missed it at all.'

When everyone was sorted out with the right plates and they'd started tucking in, Jess took up the conversation again.

'I think you did exactly the right thing – in the shop just then,' she said to Caz. 'Melissa's a coward, really. She soon backs down if you show her you're not scared, and then she'll leave you alone.'

'Anyway, you've got us now,' Lauren said. 'You don't have to sit with Melissa and Ashley at break any more. Unless you want to, that is.'

'No way!' Caz retorted, feeling a warm, happy glow running through her body.

'You'll have to meet Nikki and Sunny properly, too,' Jess told her. 'They're in my class. Sunny's a boffin but she's ever so nice, and Nikki's heavily into sport. You know, they came round with us to your house when we were going bowling.'

'I'm sorry I didn't come out with you that time,' Caz said in a rush, before she could lose her nerve. 'I was just feeling a bit shy, I suppose.'

'That's OK,' Lauren replied, pushing back her empty plate. She sucked up the last of her milkshake with a noise like a gurgling drain. 'How are you settling in, anyway? Got every-thing sorted out?'

Caz shook her head. 'My room's really small,

and it's still full of cardboard boxes,' she con-
fessed. 'I just don't know where to put everything.'

Lauren's face lit up. 'Can I help?' she said. 'I
love fixing up rooms and making them look
different. I want to be an interior designer when
I'm older.'

'That would be great,' Caz answered, not
quite believing her luck. 'I'm not doing anything tomorrow, if you're free then.'

'Sure!' Lauren smiled. 'How about you guys?'
she added, turning to Michelle and Jess.

Michelle was going out with her mum on
Sunday but Jess was free, so it was all arranged.

'See you tomorrow,' Caz said, when the plates
and glasses were empty and they had to give up
their table in the busy café. She caught her
mother's eye as everyone got up to leave and
gave her a dazzling smile. Suddenly, everything
had changed. She wasn't on her own after all!

The next morning, Caz lay on her bed, deep in a
book that Becky had recommended. She was
actually quite enjoying it. Her mother and step-

father were reading the papers downstairs and the house was quiet, apart from the blare of a radio coming from Natalie's room.

'I hate you, mama, and everything you do!' screeched the singer. 'I hate your ugly face and your ugly butt too!'

Caz sighed, trying to ignore the music. Natalie usually didn't surface till lunchtime on Sundays, but today she was going to the market with her friend Jools. Caz's mum had managed to worm that information out of Natalie when she'd appeared unexpectedly at breakfast. And then, horror of horrors, Jackie had suggested that they might like to take Caz with them! She'd nearly died on the spot, and Natalie hadn't looked too pleased about it either. Luckily, Caz had been able to say that Lauren and Jess were coming round to sort out her room, which let everybody off the hook.

Caz still felt uncomfortable around her step-sister. Natalie looked so fierce, with her black-rimmed eyes and her weird clothes. Caz had no idea what to talk to her about, and she was convinced Natalie thought she was a creep.

She probably didn't like being part of this new family any more than Caz did, but they were all in the same boat, weren't they? Caz had to share her mother with Michael, and that wasn't easy either. At least they'd had more room in the last house, and she'd been away at boarding school in the term time. Then at Christmas her real dad had said he couldn't pay her school fees any more, Michael had lost his job, and they'd ended up all lumped together here.

Caz was jolted out of her thoughts by the sound of the doorbell. 'I'll get that!' she shouted, laying down her book and thundering down the stairs.

Lauren and Jess were standing on the doorstep, as she'd expected, so Caz took them straight up to her room.

'See?' she said, pointing at the dingy walls and tatty cream carpet. 'It's so boring! Like living in a hotel room, except there's nowhere to put anything. My wardrobe won't fit through the door, and all my clothes are still in boxes.'

'It's perfect!' Lauren said, pushing a cardboard box aside and pacing round the room.

'How d'you work that out?' Caz asked, looking at her in surprise.

'Because you can do so much with it!' Lauren replied enthusiastically. 'And I'm sure there's a way of fitting all your stuff in if we think about it.'

'She's really good – trust me,' Jess told Caz, nodding her head in Lauren's direction. 'Her own bedroom's amazing. I'm just here to carry out orders.'

The front door slammed below them, and Jess looked out of the window into the street. 'Who are those two?' she asked, turning to Caz with a grin.

'That's Natalie, my stepsister – the one on the right,' she replied, peering over Jess's shoulder and giving a little shiver. 'She's going to the market with her friend.'

Natalie had gelled her short black hair up in spikes at the front, and she was wearing a dark green tie-dyed T-shirt and a pair of baggy black jeans that ballooned out over her clumpy Doc Martens. She looked even more frightening than usual.

'Woo, scary!' Jess giggled. 'You wouldn't want to mess with those two. What's she like?'

'I don't really know,' Caz replied with a shrug. 'I've never spent that much time with her. She normally stays with her mum in the holiday and I was away at boarding school in the term time. Mum's always trying to suck up to her – that's probably why she let Natalie have the biggest bedroom. It's not working, though. Natalie doesn't speak to her either.'

A gleam came into Jess's eye. 'Why don't we go and look round her room?' she suggested to Caz. 'I bet you've never been in there, have you?'

'Course not!' Caz said, half appalled and half excited at the idea. Natalie spent hours in her room, and Caz had often wondered exactly what she did in there. But did she have the nerve to find out?

'Come on,' Jess said, taking her arm and steering her towards the door. 'They'll be gone for ages. Let's leave Lauren to work out her master plan and have some fun.'

'D'you mind, Lauren?' Caz asked, but she just shook her curly hair in reply and waved them away, already deep in thought.

'We might get some ideas,' Caz whispered, as she and Jess crept out of her room and creaked open the door of Natalie's. 'You know, about how to arrange things.'

'I don't think so,' Jess replied, staring round once they were inside. 'It's even more of a tip than yours!'

Natalie's bedroom floor looked like the surface of some strange planet. Her clothes were heaped over it in great dark mounds, with towers of books stacked between them like stalagmites. A length of black velvet had been flung over the curtain pole, and a green lava lamp cast a sickly glow in one corner of the room. Wispy smoke from smouldering sticks of incense spiralled up through the gloom.

'It's just like Eddie's room,' Jess whispered, nudging Caz's arm. 'He's my oldest brother. We ought to get them together – they'd make a great couple!'

Caz smiled at the thought

as she gazed around. 'I don't know what she's doing with my wardrobe,' she said jealously. 'Not hanging her clothes in it, that's for sure.'

'Hey, look at those!' Jess said suddenly, grabbing Caz's arm and pointing. A pair of spike-heeled red leather boots were propped against the wall in a far corner of the room. 'They are so wicked!' she breathed, threading her way through piles of junk and holding up the boots for Caz to see.

'Incredible,' Caz agreed – and then her eyes widened. 'What are you doing?' she gasped, horrified.

'Trying them on, of course,' Jess replied, squashing her foot into one of the boots. 'I reckon they're only a couple of sizes too big.'

'You've got a nerve!' Caz gasped, giggling nervously. 'Natalie'd go spare if she saw you.'

'Well, she won't see me, will she?' Jess said, cramming on the other boot and looking at herself in a mirror on the open wardrobe door. 'Now, what do you think? Do they look good with these trousers or what?' And she minced off on a circuit of the room.

'Your turn now,' she told Caz when she'd come back, starting to tug at one of the boots. 'Here, you couldn't give me a hand to take them off, could you? They're a bit tight round the ankle.'

'Sit on the bed,' Caz suggested. 'I'll pull.'

Eventually, after a few seconds' struggle, she staggered back with one of the boots in her hands.

'Think I can manage this one,' Jess said, wrestling with the other. 'Go on – give them a try! They'll look fantastic with your pink T-shirt.'

'OK,' Caz giggled, hopping around on one leg as she squeezed the boot on. She'd never have dared if she'd been on her own, but somehow she felt safe with Jess beside her.

And then suddenly they both heard a sound that was so unbelievable, and so terrifying, it took a few seconds to register.

Natalie was coming up the stairs.

'Forgotten my Travelcard,' she was growling, in answer to some twittered question from Caz's mum.

Caz and Jess stared at each other, dumb with horror.

'We've got to get them off!' Caz hissed desperately, wrenching at the scarlet boot on her right leg. Natalie was at the top of the stairs now – in another few seconds she'd be in the room.

'No time!' Jess replied. Hopping awkwardly on the other red boot, she hustled Caz over to the window, flung back the black velvet curtain and dived behind it, pulling Caz in after her.

They clung together in the narrow hiding place. Caz could feel her legs trembling, and Jess's fingers were damp and sweaty on her bare arm. The curtain smelt of incense and the atmosphere behind it was stuffy and airless. On the other side of the thin material, they could hear Natalie stomping up and down like a wild animal in its lair, knocking things over and swearing under her breath as she looked for her Travelcard.

Jess squeezed Caz's arm for a second, then glanced meaningfully downwards at her feet. Caz raised her eyebrows, not quite getting the picture. She looked down too, and then couldn't hold back a gasp of shock as she understood what Jess was trying to tell her. Apart from one red boot each, their feet were bare. Her espadrilles and Jess's trainers were lying among heaps of junk in the middle of the bedroom floor.

Oh please, don't let Natalie find them, Caz prayed silently, trying to flatten herself even more tightly against the window. I'll never come in this room ever again, I promise, as long as I live. I'll never bother Natalie, or talk to her, or even look at her . . .

A loud crash beyond the curtain made them both jump, and then they heard a clash of coat hangers. Natalie must have flung open the wardrobe door; now she was searching through her clothes. So she has hung *some* of them up, Caz thought, and had to bite her lip to stop herself giggling. Hysterical laughter bubbled up inside her, despite the desperate situation they were in, and threatened to burst out. She tried to think stern thoughts, to damp it down. How could Natalie not notice their shoes? And whatever would they say if – when – she eventually drew back the curtain? It was too awful to imagine.

Then Caz became aware that Jess's whole body was shaking. She'd got the giggles too – her face was turning red with the effort of keeping them in, and she was digging her fingernails into Caz's arm. Caz looked up at the ceiling, then down at the floor – anywhere rather than catch Jess's eye. She knew she didn't stand a chance of controlling herself if she did. Then they would both be doomed.

And then, when Caz thought Jess was about to explode and she was going to bite right through her lip, they heard something that brought them hope.

'At last!' Natalie muttered. She clomped over to the door and called downstairs, 'Coming, Jools! I found my card in a jacket pocket.'

They couldn't hang on to make sure Natalie had really gone. Pulling aside the curtain, Caz and Jess staggered out, still clinging to each other. They half-hopped, half-fell over to the bed and collapsed on to it, not able to do anything but laugh until the tears streamed down their cheeks.

'*There* you are!' Lauren said, when Caz and Jess eventually made their way back across the landing, clutching their shoes. 'I was beginning to wonder what had happened.'

They took turns telling Lauren the whole story, giggling all over again now they were back in the safety of Caz's bedroom.

'Thank goodness I didn't come with you!' Lauren breathed, horrified, when they'd finished. 'I would have died on the spot!'

'So how have you been getting on in here?' Caz asked, wiping her eyes as she looked round the room. It was bare, apart from the bed and a chest of drawers – Lauren had dragged all the cardboard boxes out on to the landing.

'Well, see those two alcoves on either side of the bed?' Lauren said with a gleam in her eye. Caz nodded. 'If you put a pole across one of them,' she went on, 'you could hang your clothes up there, with maybe a curtain or something across the front to keep them hidden. And you could put shelves on the other side, for books, or baskets to store all your bits and pieces. What do you think?'

'Great!' Caz said, beginning to picture how her room might look.

'See?' Jess said, sitting up on the bed. 'I told you Lauren was the business.'

'And there's nearly a whole tin of blue paint left over from when Mum and I painted the kitchen,' Lauren went on, pushing up her sleeves in a business-like way. 'I'm sure she wouldn't mind letting us have it.'

'Paint the room?' Caz said. 'What – us? That's a bit ambitious, isn't it? I was just thinking of tidying everything away.'

'Nah, we can do better than that,' Lauren said,

gazing around again. 'All we need to do is wash the walls down first – there aren't any cracks or anything. It won't take that long with the three of us. Maybe you'd better check with your mum that she doesn't mind, while I go back home and fetch the paint. Is that OK? Not being too bossy, am I?'

'Whatever you say!' Caz replied, happy to put herself in Lauren's hands. After all, her room could hardly end up looking worse than it did already, could it?

Jackie thought it was a great idea for the three of them to paint the room, as long as they put on some old clothes and spread newspaper all over the floor. 'We can't let Lauren's mum give us the paint, though,' she said anxiously. 'I'll see if she'll accept some money – it's the least we can do.'

'Do you girls want a hand?' Michael asked, folding up the newspaper.

'Oh no, it's OK, thanks,' Caz answered quickly. It was nice of him to offer, but they'd have much more fun on their own.

'Well, in that case I'll get the brushes and

everything ready for you,' he said, standing up. 'And while I think of it, I found some planks of wood in the shed yesterday. I could cut them to size and fit shelves up in the alcove for you, if that's what you want.'

'Brilliant! Thanks,' Caz said in surprise. She had no idea he was such a handyman.

By the time Lauren came back with the paint, Jess and Caz were already wearing a couple of Michael's old shirts and sloshing soapy water all over Caz's bedroom walls. The radio was playing and it was quite cosy, really. Much better to be doing something, Caz thought to herself, than hanging around feeling depressed.

'It's really nice of you to help me,' she said to the other two. 'I'd never have done all this on my own.'

'But it's fun,' Lauren replied, spreading a dustsheet over the bed. 'We're going to make this room look so cool! Besides, I owe you a favour, remember? After you saved me from Melissa.'

'Oh, Melissa,' Caz groaned. She wasn't exactly

looking forward to seeing her in school the next day.

'Don't worry about her,' Jess said confidently, flicking soapsuds in Caz's direction. 'After what we've just been through, Melissa's a doddle!'

They worked away steadily for the next couple of hours, painting and chatting to each other. Jess kept stopping to dance to her favourite song on the radio or flop down on the bed for a rest, but she was so funny it was impossible to be cross with her. Caz's mum brought up a tray of lemonade and crisps to keep them going, and Michael kept putting his head round the door to see how they were getting on. Besides the wood for shelves, he'd also found an old broom handle in the shed.

'I'll fix it up in the alcove when you've finished painting,' he said, showing it to Caz. 'That'll be just the thing for hanging up your clothes.'

At last Caz put

down her paintbrush, rubbed her aching shoulders, and looked round the room. 'I can't believe it!' she said. 'The whole place looks completely different!'

Every centimetre of her bedroom walls glowed a lovely soft blue. The room had been transformed into somewhere cosy and inviting, instead of the dingy bolt-hole it had been before.

'It's a great colour, isn't it?' Lauren said, starting to tidy up the sheets of newspaper that they'd spread over the floor. 'And this is just the beginning! You could make it look even better with matching curtains and cushions and things. Maybe lilac, or pale green. They'd look good with this blue.'

'Maybe,' Caz said doubtfully. She could just imagine what her mum would say about that! *'You'll have to make do with what you've got for a while, Carrie. We're meant to be pulling in our horns, remember?'*

Lauren seemed to guess what she was thinking. 'You don't have spend a fortune,' she said, sitting back on her heels. She reached over to finger one of the cream curtains which they'd taken down to keep clear of the paint. 'I bet you could dye these, you know.'

'Perhaps you could tie-dye them,' Jess suggested, pouring herself some more lemonade. 'You know – like Natalie's T-shirt. Two colours, like blue and purple, with circles or stripes all over them.'

'That would be fantastic!' Caz said, inspired. Now they'd begun to work on her room, it was easier to see what it could look like eventually. With a little more effort and imagination, it might become somewhere she'd actually want to spend her time. She could hang crystals at the window, maybe, and put up a pinboard for photos and cards. And her tatty old chest of drawers – that could be painted too. She was on a roll!

'Shall we start to bring everything back?' Jess asked, putting down her glass. 'Most of the paint's dry now, except for this last wall.'

'I suppose so,' Caz sighed, coming back down to earth with a bump. There still wasn't enough room to store everything she'd brought from the last house. 'I've got too much stuff, that's my problem,' she said, dragging in the biggest of the boxes. 'And most of it I never wear.'

'I know!' Lauren said, following on behind her with another box. 'Why don't we hold a garage sale? We had one last summer and half the people in our year came – it was great.'

'Yeah, it was,' Jess chimed in. 'My older sister sold a load of stuff she'd grown out of. Mum was mad, though – she said they were all things she was keeping for me! Maybe I'm going to get something new this summer for a change.'

'That's a great idea!' Caz said, thinking it over. She began rummaging through the box. There was the lime green T-shirt dress that had never really suited her in the first place, and those flowery leggings she'd grown out of last summer. There must be at least three pairs of jeans she didn't wear any more, either, especially now she was into flares. She could have a good clear out and streamline her wardrobe.

There was something else in the back of her mind that she wanted to organise, too. Whilst they'd been painting, she'd come up with a plan to invite Michelle, Sunny and Nikki – with Jess and Lauren, of course – over for her birthday next weekend. It would be the ideal chance for her to get to know them as well as she was getting to know Lauren and Jess. Her room might be too small for a sleepover, but there were plenty of other things they could do, and having the five of them over together would be bound to turn into a party. She'd invite them all at school tomorrow.

Caz looked round her beautiful blue room and smiled. Things were going to work out just fine!

'Not hiding from me, are you?'

Caz's stomach did a double somersault at the sound of Melissa's voice. The bell had gone for break on Monday and Lauren and Michelle had already rushed out to the playground to meet up with Jess and the others.

Stand up for yourself, Caz thought, remembering what Jess had said. Don't show Melissa you're scared, whatever happens. 'Course I'm not hiding,' she said, looking her straight in the eye. 'Why would I do that?'

'You know why,' Melissa hissed. 'I told Ashley what you did on Saturday and she thinks you've got a nerve, too. Don't you, Ash?'

Ashley nodded. 'Yeah, a real nerve,' she said, narrowing her eyes and sticking out her chin.

'We think you should apologise,' Melissa said softly, leaning forward and grabbing Caz's arm tightly.

Caz wrenched her arm away, suddenly so furious she didn't have to pretend to be brave. 'What are you talking about?' she said. 'Look what you did to me!' And she rolled up her sleeve and shoved her arm back in Melissa's face. Although she'd been rubbing antiseptic cream on the scratch marks, they still looked red and sore.

Even Melissa looked surprised to see the damage she'd caused. She took a step backwards, which gave Caz confidence.

'That's evidence,' she went on, not caring who heard. 'If you come near me again, I'll go straight to Mrs Ryder and show her what you did!'

'Oh, will you?' Melissa sneered, smiling at Ashley. 'Are you going to tell your mummy too?'

'Yes, why not?' Caz said, pulling her sleeve back down. 'And while I'm about it, I'll tell her that I saw you shoplifting as well. I bet the police would be interested to hear that.'

'You wouldn't dare!' Melissa said, turning

pale. Ashley scratched her head blankly and tried to follow what was going on.

'Try me,' Caz retorted. She folded her arms and stared Melissa full in the face.

'Come on, Ash,' Melissa muttered, after a few seconds. 'Let's not hang around here. Something stinks, and for once it's not you.'

Caz watched as they went away, arm in arm. Somehow, she knew Melissa wouldn't be bothering her any more. She'd won that particular battle.

'There you are!' Lauren said as soon as she caught sight of Caz in the playground. 'What was that all about?'

'Nothing really,' Caz replied airily. 'Just sorting a few things out with Melissa. Come on, let's go and find the others.'

Jess, Michelle, Nikki and Sunny were in a huddle in the far corner of the playground. At first, they just wanted to talk to Caz about Melissa and everything that had happened over the weekend, but soon she was able to steer the conversation round to Lauren's suggestion of the garage sale.

'That's such a brilliant idea,' Sunny said, putting an arm round Lauren's waist and swinging her around. 'We needn't just have clothes, either – we could sell CDs and jewellery and books too. Are we going to have it at your house?'

'Can you all come round to mine?' Caz asked, wanting to show Sunny she wasn't as stand-offish as she must have seemed the last time they'd met. 'You could see the fantastic job we did on my bedroom.'

'That would be great!' Sunny said, giving her a smile. 'When shall it be, then? How about this Saturday?'

'Well, that's another thing,' Caz said cautiously. She looked into the ring of faces around her – Jess with her auburn hair and freckles, Lauren's mass of curls, Sunny's clever dark eyes, Nikki looking even blonder beside her, and Michelle, hanging back a little at the edge of the group. She hadn't known them for very long, but she felt sure she could trust them.

'It's my birthday on Saturday,' she said, deciding to take the plunge. 'I was wondering if you could all come over. My room's too small for a sleepover, but maybe we could do something else. What do you think?'

'Sure,' Jess said easily. 'That would be great! Perhaps we could go ice skating or bowling – something like that.'

'I'm free,' Lauren said. 'I'd love to come!'

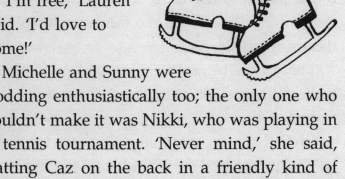

Michelle and Sunny were nodding enthusiastically too; the only one who couldn't make it was Nikki, who was playing in a tennis tournament. 'Never mind,' she said, patting Caz on the back in a friendly kind of way. 'I'm sure there'll be another time.'

'So why don't we have the sale on Thursday, after school?' Sunny suggested. 'That'll give us a few days to get our stuff together and spread the word around. What do you think?'

'Great!' said Jess. 'Sale on Thursday, party on Saturday – that's everything sorted.'

Caz beamed, feeling on top of the world. Everything had gone much more smoothly than she could've hoped – it must be because they were all so nice and easy to be with. Suddenly she wanted her party to be extra special, as a kind of thank you. 'I know,' she said excitedly. 'Let's go to a theme park on Saturday! That's what we did for my birthday last year, and it was brilliant!'

'Wicked!' Jess said, her eyes lighting up. 'We could go on all the scariest rides. I love theme parks!' Then she corrected herself. 'Well, I've only been once before, but I loved it then.'

'Oh, it's such a pain I can't be there,' Nikki grumbled. 'You lot are going to have a great time, and I have to play in some stupid tennis match.'

'I'll ask Mum tonight,' Caz said happily. 'I'm sure she won't mind taking us.'

But when Caz tackled her mother in the kitchen after school that afternoon, Jackie dropped a bombshell. 'I'm sorry, love,' she sighed. 'We're on an economy drive now, remember? There's no way I can afford to take a whole group of you off on some expensive outing.'

For a second, Caz couldn't believe what she'd

just heard. 'What?' she said, letting the teaspoon she'd been fiddling with clatter on to the table. 'But last year—'

'Last year it cost me a fortune,' her mum said, wincing. 'We just don't have that kind of money to spare at the moment. I'm sorry, love. I can take a couple of you to the cinema, but that's about it.'

'I've invited everyone now, though!' Caz said, her voice rising in despair.

'Then you'll just have to un-invite them,' her mother replied sharply, dropping some teabags into the pot. 'You shouldn't have gone making arrangements without checking with me first. You know I'd do anything to make your birthday special, Carrie, love, but a theme park is out of the question this year. That's all there is to it.'

Caz pushed her chair back. 'I thought it was too good to be true,' she said bitterly. 'Just when I was beginning to make friends, something has to go and ruin it. I'm going to look a complete idiot now, aren't I? No one's going to want to know me after this!' And she stormed out of the room, slamming the door so hard it bounced back on its hinges.

No matter how much Caz pleaded with her mother over tea that evening, and breakfast the next morning, Jackie wouldn't change her mind. They just didn't have the money for an expensive party this year, and that was that.

'But I really need to make friends at my new school, Mum!' Caz tried as a desperate last resort. 'I don't know the others that well, and I want them to like me. It's not as though I can invite them to a sleepover, is it? Not in my titchy room.'

'If they're worth making friends with, they'll understand,' her mum said firmly. 'And if they'll only like you if you take them to a theme park, they're not worth bothering with.'

Caz bit her fingernails anxiously. She knew Jess and Lauren and the others weren't like that but, all the same, she couldn't bear the thought of breaking the news that her party was going to be one big non-event. She could just imagine what the girls at her last school would have said if she'd arranged a party and then cancelled it the next day. And what would they do on Saturday afternoon instead? Sit round eating crisps and watching videos?

Over the next couple of days, she tried to bring herself to tell her new friends that there'd been a change of plan – but somehow the moment never seemed quite right. Being part of their group felt great and she wanted to hang on to that warm, safe feeling for just a little longer. I'll tell them soon, she kept promising herself. Perhaps if they know me better, they won't think I'm such an idiot when they find out what a mess I've made of things. She wasn't sleeping well, though, and whenever she thought about her birthday she had a sick feeling in the pit of her stomach.

Tuesday came and went, then Wednesday, and before Caz could blink it was Thursday. She knew she should have talked to the others before they came round to her house after school that day, but everyone was so busy discussing the sale that she didn't get a chance. Someone was bound to bring up the subject of theme parks that afternoon. What if her mother overheard?

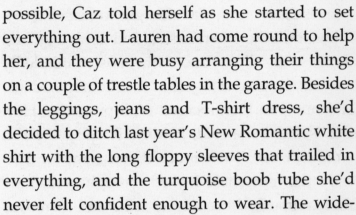

I'm just going to have to keep Mum in the house as much as possible, Caz told herself as she started to set everything out. Lauren had come round to help her, and they were busy arranging their things on a couple of trestle tables in the garage. Besides the leggings, jeans and T-shirt dress, she'd decided to ditch last year's New Romantic white shirt with the long floppy sleeves that trailed in everything, and the turquoise boob tube she'd never felt confident enough to wear. The wide-legged shorts went out too (mega-unflattering), and the drawstring skirt that made her look fat.

'What's all this, then?' Natalie asked, pausing as she walked home from sixth-form college.

'We're having a sale,' Caz answered distract-
edly. 'Clothes, books – that kind of thing. There
are some other girls from school coming round
soon.'

Natalie grunted, raised her eyebrows and
went into the house.

Perhaps I should tell Lauren now, while no
one else is around, Caz thought to herself. No –
I'll wait till the others arrive, and get it over and
done with all at once. She absent-mindedly
stroked the green silky shirt that Lauren had just
laid out, and then focused on it properly. 'Hey,
this is nice!' she said, holding it up to see if it
would fit her. 'How much d'you want for it?'

By the time she'd looked through everything
that Lauren had brought to sell – and there was
some very tasty gear – she'd forgotten the carefully
prepared speech she'd been rehearsing so many
times. And when Jess, Sunny, Michelle and Nikki
eventually did arrive, they were in the middle of a
whole group of girls from their class. There was no
way she could get them on their own.

The only consolation was that Caz's mum
agreed to stay in the kitchen and let them get

on with everything by themselves – and that the sale itself was a huge success. The surprise hit of the afternoon was Natalie, who suddenly appeared with a huge bundle of clothes in her arms.

'D'you mind if I join in?' she asked Caz. 'It's a good idea, this.'

Natalie's table was the main attraction. People fought each other for her zingy crop tops and stretchy Lycra skirts, and soon she went back upstairs again to fetch yet more clothes and about fifteen pairs of shoes and sandals.

'I suppose this is all the stuff she used to wear before she turned into a Goth,' Jess murmured in Caz's ear. 'Do you think we should make an offer for her kinky boots?'

Caz giggled, and then pounced on a wicked paisley T-shirt she'd just spotted in the heap. 'Can I buy this?' she asked Natalie rather nervously. 'How much is it?'

'Go on, you can have that,' Natalie answered, winking at her. 'Special discount for family. After all, I'm raking in the money here.' Caz nearly dropped dead with shock.

Eventually, everything that was going to be sold had been snapped up, and the leftovers were stuffed into dustbin liners for the charity shop. All the customers had gone home, and Michelle, Jess, Nikki and Sunny were helping Lauren and Caz clear up. Now I have to say something, Caz said to herself. She was just wondering how on earth to begin when the matter was taken out of her hands.

'Hey, I nearly forgot!' Nikki said to her, after they'd dragged the trestle tables back against the garage wall. 'My match has been cancelled on Saturday, so I can come to your party after all. That's great, isn't it?'

'But how are we all going to fit in one car?' Lauren worried. 'Perhaps I should see if my mum can take some of us.'

Caz took a deep breath. 'There's something I've got to tell you,' she said awkwardly, raising her voice so that they could all hear. 'I don't really know how to say this, but we can't go to a theme park after all. I'm sorry.'

It was so difficult for her to come out with it,

just like that, but at last she'd done it. She'd told them. The butterflies in her stomach stopped fluttering quite so wildly.

'Why not?' Nikki asked, stuffing everything she'd bought into a carrier bag. 'What's the problem?'

Caz hesitated for a second. Perhaps she could say that her mum hated crowds, or thought roller coasters were dangerous. No, she might as well tell the truth. 'Because we can't afford it,' she said miserably. 'Things are really tough at home at the moment. We'll be better off if my mum can get a job, but I can't have much of a party this year. Sorry.'

For the first time, she dared to lift her eyes. None of the others were staring at her, or exchanging those sly glances that meant they'd be sneering behind her back later on. In fact, they didn't look that bothered. Caz couldn't believe it! She'd told the truth, and the sky hadn't fallen down after all.

'I *thought* it would cost a fortune,' Jess said. 'Mum says Matt and I are going to have to wait till the others leave home before she'll take us to a theme park. Matt's my twin brother,' she explained for Caz's benefit.

'Michelle's boyfriend,' Sunny said, with a straight face.

'Will you stop going on about that?' Michelle shouted, starting to chase her, so Caz guessed maybe that wasn't quite true.

'We can still come round to your house, though, can't we?' Lauren asked.

'Well, yes – of course,' Caz stuttered, falling over her words. 'If you want to, that is. But you know there isn't room for a sleepover, don't you? We could hire a video or something, I suppose.'

'Come on, we can do better than that!' Sunny said, tucking her long black hair behind one ear. 'This is your birthday we're talking about. And it's Saturday night, remember?'

'I know,' Jess broke in excitedly. 'Got it! Why don't we organise a surprise party for you? We are the best at parties, believe me. Just wait – we'll think up something good!'

'You won't have to do a thing,' Lauren told Caz. 'Leave it to us – we'll arrange everything. Jess, you're a genius!'

'Are you sure you don't mind? Not going to the theme park, I mean,' Caz asked. She felt dizzy with relief, so light-headed she could float up into the air. 'Oh, I've been so worried about telling you!'

'Don't be silly,' Lauren said matter-of-factly. 'It doesn't matter where we go. As long as we're together, we'll have fun.'

Caz was so happy she could have hugged them all. So Lauren, Sunny, Jess, Michelle and Nikki really were her friends. They didn't care how much money her parents had, or what kind of place she lived in – they just liked her for who she was.

'Yes,' she said, breaking into a wide grin. 'Of course we will!'

'Happy birthday, love,' Caz's mum said, putting her head round the bedroom door. 'I was wondering when you were going to surface. Here, I've brought up your cards.'

'Thanks, Mum,' Caz said eagerly, sitting up in bed. She'd been dreading her birthday for so long that now it seemed extra sweet. She was determined to enjoy every minute.

'Your room is so lovely now,' her mother said, settling herself on the bed and looking round while Caz flicked through her cards. As promised, Michael had fitted shelves into the alcove beside Caz's bed. He'd even bought some lilac gloss paint and decorated all the woodwork – shelves, windowframe, door, and Caz's chest of drawers. It looked stunning, and Caz had been really touched.

'Yeah, it's great,' Caz said absent-mindedly. She looked up at her mother, disappointed. 'Are

these all the cards? There's nothing from Dad, is there?'

'Oh well, you know what he's like,' Jackie Bennett replied, patting the mound Caz's feet made under the duvet. 'It will probably arrive next week.'

'But he *always* sends a card,' Caz grumbled, slitting open one of the envelopes in her hand. She and her dad had a running joke – they always gave each other cards with the soppiest rhymes they could find. Her birthday wouldn't be the same without one.

'Well, don't give up just yet. You never know,' her mother answered vaguely.

Caz tried not to mind. After all, she had plenty of other things to look forward to today – particularly her surprise party. She knew Jess and Lauren had talked to her mum in the kitchen for ages the night before, after the sale. All Caz could find out was that the party was going to start around five – everything else was being kept strictly secret.

'You'll find out soon enough,' was all Jackie Bennett would say, no matter how much Caz nagged.

'Good old Gran!' Caz said now, holding up a postal order which had fallen out of her grandmother's card. 'Can we go shopping today, Mum?' she asked, choosing another card. This one was from her mum and Michael, and had a photo of Caz pasted on to a picture of her favourite pop group. Caz grinned. Her mother always made funny cards.

'We'll see,' Jackie replied, getting up from the bed. 'Breakfast first, anyway. I'll put some bacon under the grill.'

'Thanks, Mum!' Caz said, giving her mother a hug. Bacon sarnies were another birthday tradition. 'And thanks for the card – it's great!'

A pile of presents was waiting on the kitchen table when Caz came downstairs. There was a bottle of black nail varnish from Natalie, who'd left it there the night before in case she wasn't up in the morning. And her stepdad had given her a spotlight she could clip on to the shelves, for reading in bed. Her mum had got loads of little things – karma beads, pink and purple bangles, lavender oil for the bath, a photo frame and a mirror – and a fantastic purple beaded curtain that she'd found in the Oxfam shop.

'I thought you could hang it over the alcove where your clothes are. It's good, isn't it?' Jackie said proudly. 'Michael can fix it up for you.'

'Brilliant!' Caz said, giving her mother another bear hug. 'Thanks for everything, Mum.' She steeled herself and gave her stepfather a quick hug, too. 'Thanks, Michael. For the light, and for doing all that work in my room. I really appreciate it.'

Caz was just getting dressed half an hour later when the doorbell rang. 'Answer that, will you, love?' her mother called up from the kitchen. 'I've got my hands full.'

Caz was in too good a mood to moan, so she padded downstairs in her socks and opened the door. A tall man with sandy hair was standing on the doorstep, his hands in his pockets.

'Dad!' she shouted in amazement, flinging herself into his arms. 'What are you doing here?'

'Come to deliver your card in person,' he grinned, disentangling himself and handing Caz a pink envelope with flowers all over it. 'And to whisk you off for a day of shopping – or whatever else your heart desires.'

'That's brilliant!' Caz said, her face lighting up. 'You mean we've got the whole day together?'

'That's right,' her dad replied. 'I just have to get you back by five, your mother tells me.'

'Great!' Caz exclaimed, tearing open her card. On the front was a picture of a little girl with a huge head and lots of blonde curls tied up in a gingham scarf. She was carrying a kitten in a basket and bending down to smell some flowers while butter-flies fluttered round her head. It looked promising. Inside, the rhyme was written in flowing script:

You grow more lovely every year,
Precious, sweetest daughter dear!
And so on this, your special day,
What joy it brings us all to say,
Happy birthday! And, in the year to come,
May all your days be filled with laughter and fun!

'Not bad,' Caz said critically. 'I like the way the last line doesn't quite fit.'

'Yes, I thought that was good too,' her father agreed. 'And it doesn't quite rhyme, either. Don't lose your present now, will you?' Two twenty-pound notes had been tucked into the card.

'Oh, thanks, Dad!' Caz said, hugging him tightly. The money was great, but the fact that they had a day together on their own was best of all.

After that, things just got better and better. Caz and her dad shopped till they dropped, went to a swanky café for lunch, and then saw the latest film everyone was talking about. Although she was having a great time, Caz started glancing at her watch towards the end of it. She couldn't begin to imagine what Jess and the others were planning for her party.

When her dad delivered her back home, though, the house was quiet. 'Where is everyone?' Caz asked her mum in the hall. 'Haven't they come round yet?'

'Just go and put those bags in your room,' Jackie replied, hustling Caz up the stairs. 'Come on, quickly now!'

Caz went upstairs, full of misgivings. Perhaps nothing was going to happen after all. Maybe the others had decided a party was too much trouble. Or maybe they were all hiding in her room, ready to burst out when she opened the door? She pushed her door open gingerly, and peeped inside.

There was no one in the room. Hanging on a length of silver string from the ceiling, though, was a big silver star. Caz dropped her carrier bags and went over to look at it. She turned the star over, and silver writing shone out against the black card on the other side.

What? Caz thought to herself.
A party in the garden?
How come?
Her heart began
to pound with
excitement, and
she looked
quickly round
the room
for any more clues.

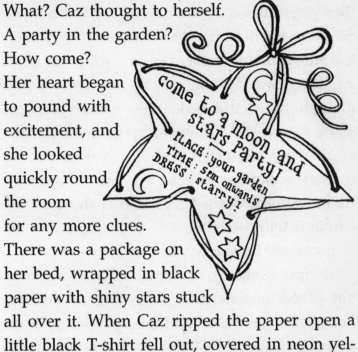

come to a moon and
stars party!
PLACE: your garden
TIME: 5pm onwards
DRESS: starry!

There was a package on
her bed, wrapped in black
paper with shiny stars stuck
all over it. When Caz ripped the paper open a
little black T-shirt fell out, covered in neon yellow stars and blue and green planets. Another
silver foil star was pinned to it, with silver
writing on the back which read, 'Happy birthday, from Lauren'.

'Better get changed, love, or you'll be late,' said
her mum, smiling at her from the doorway.

Hurriedly, Caz pulled the T-shirt on. She
didn't have any starry trousers, so a pair of black
ones would have to do. After she'd wriggled into

them, she rushed across the landing to the bath-room and flung open the window overlooking the garden. At first she couldn't quite make out what she was looking at. There seemed to be paper bags on either side of the garden path, for some reason. And then she spotted the garden shed. Huge silver stars had been tacked all over t, and a bunch of gold and silver balloons uttered from the weathervane at the top. She rieked with excitement and hurtled down the stairs as fast as she possibly could.

'Surprise!' shouted Lauren and Jess, bursting out of the shed when Caz wrenched open the door, Michelle, Nikki and Sunny close behind.

'I don't believe this!' Caz gasped as she stared round the inside of the shed. 'What have you done? This is fantastic!'

The last time she'd seen the shed, it had been full of cardboard boxes and all kinds of other rubbish. Now it had been completely cleared out, and she was surprised to see just how big the place was. That wasn't all – the windows had been blacked out with black paper and glow-in-the-dark stars had been stuck all over the walls, with more silver foil stars hanging down from the ceiling. One orange flashlight shed a dim glow, and sleeping bags and cushions all over the floor turned the shed into a magical, secret hideaway.

'Haven't we done a great job?' Jess said, hopping up and down with excitement. 'It took us ages to clear all the junk out, but your mum helped too, and Michael took everything to the tip. Don't you think this is a cool place?'

'It's perfect!' Caz said, her eyes shining. 'And I love this T-shirt, Lauren! Thanks so much.'

'I painted it myself,' Lauren told her proudly. 'It glows in the dark – see?'

'And there's something else,' Sunny said eagerly. 'We heard your mum and Michael talking together and they said that—'

'—now we've put such a lot of effort into making the shed look so nice, it's a pity to fill it up with boxes again,' Michelle finished triumphantly. 'You can have it for your own special place, when you feel like getting away from everyone.'

'Or when you feel like inviting your friends round,' Nikki said hopefully, and everyone burst out laughing. They crowded round Caz with their presents. Michelle had bought her a pair of star earrings, Sunny  had found a little round box with a moon and stars painted on the lid, and Nikki had come up with a pair of funky star-shaped sunglasses. Jess presented Caz with a 'Stars of the Seventies' tape, and everyone groaned.

'Don't you think that's clever?' she asked, disappointed. 'I was really pleased when I saw it. And look – I've brought along a battery tape recorder, so we can play it.'

'Let's put it on,' Caz said happily. 'It's a great present, Jess. Thanks!'

They listened to the tape – which was terrible – and gossiped and giggled until Caz's mum brought out a rug and loads of delicious starry food. There were hot dogs with stars piped on them in mustard and ketchup, toasted cheese stars for Lauren, raw carrot and cucumber stars, and cheesy moon and star biscuits. After that, there were strawberry and orange jelly stars with ice cream and, last of all, a big star cake sparkling with candles.

'Make a wish!' Lauren said, as Caz took a deep breath to blow them out.

I wish that we'll all be friends for ever, Caz thought to herself. I wish that every birthday is as wonderful as this one. I wish that my mum gets a job, and that Melissa leaves me alone from now on. I wish—

But then she ran out of breath, and had to leave her wish list at that.

'Good, it's getting dark,' Sunny said, looking out of the open shed door. 'Now we can light the lanterns.'

'I'll do that,' Caz's mum said, setting off with the matches. The paper bags Caz had noticed at first turned out to have candles inside, bedded in sand. Moon and star shapes had been cut out of the sides, too. When the candles were lit, the bags turned into glowing squares of light which cast speckled shadows across the path.

And then, to add the finishing touch, Natalie loomed up out of the darkness and made a camp fire in a ring of big stones on the rough ground beyond the shed.

'Don't get too close,' she warned severely, when the wood and coals were alight. 'After the flames die down you can toast marshmallows. But don't fool around, OK? Remember – I'll be watching!'

'Yes, Natalie,' they chorused obediently, trying not to laugh.

Much later, when they'd played loads of games of stick-in-the-mud and grandmother's footsteps by torchlight, and eaten hundreds of toasted marshmallows, and swapped endless secrets, Caz lay back on her sleeping bag beside the fire and looked up at the night sky. She could see the real moon through the branches of a tree, caught there like a big silver ball, and the real stars winking down at her from light years away.

This is the happiest day of my life, she thought to herself. And no matter how many birthdays I have, there'll never, *ever* be a party as good as this one!

If you enjoyed reading about Caz
and her party, look out for more
Party Girls books – with more free bangles
on book 3, *Sunny's Dream Team!*
And if you'd like to throw a party
like Caz's, read on . . .

THROW YOUR OWN ALL-STAR PARTY!

A moon and stars theme is a great idea for a party or sleepover. You can use stars for your invitations, decorate the room with stick-on glow stars and planets (check with an adult first that this is OK), and pile on star balloons, star lanterns, and a crescent moon and stars hanging down from the ceiling. It's easy to make party food starry, and why not decorate paper plates, cups and napkins with stick-on stars too? Your friends could bring you starry presents (especially if you drop a few hints!), and wrap them up in moon and stars paper.

Seeing stars

Here's an easy way to make a star shape. First, draw a large circle on a piece of paper with a slightly smaller circle inside it. (If you want to be really accurate, you can trace round a dinner plate and a saucer.)

Put a dot where you think the middle of the circle is, and then draw five lines out from this point to the edge of the larger circle. If you bear in mind that each segment will be slightly smaller than a quarter, it's easier to make the sections even.

Now, starting at point a, draw a line down to halfway along the inner circle segment, and then up to join point b, like this:

Carry on round the rest of the circle, and you'll end up with a five-pointed star. If some of the points are a little uneven, you can always make them wider or narrower now.

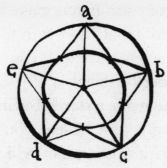

Practise star shapes a few times till you're pleased with the result, and then draw a really excellent star on to card and cut it out. This is your super star template! You can draw round it on to gold and silver card to cut out party invitations (write all the info on the back). Or you can cut out stars from cereal packets, cover them with silver foil, punch a hole in one point and hang them up from your ceiling on silver strings with a blob of Blu-tack. Cut a big crescent moon out of gold card too, or spray cereal packet card with gold paint. You can also thread gold or silver string or thin ribbon all round the edge of your star if you make holes at each inner and outer point.

Glow-in-the-dark T-shirt

If you'd like to make a starry T-shirt to wear for your party or give as a present, you'll need some glow-in-the-dark fabric paint which is sold in craft shops. Choose a black or navy T-shirt and make sure it has been washed, even if it's new. Slip a piece of card inside it so the paint won't seep through to the other side and draw on your design in chalk or a light-coloured crayon. As well as stars, you could have moons, planets or meteors – even a rocket! Then paint over your chalk designs with the special fabric paint. Leave the card inside until the paint is dry – this will take at least 24 hours. (You can hurry the process up with a hair-dryer if you're desperate!)

Eating stars

Starry food is fun to make. You can buy bright yellow American mustard (which isn't too strong!) in squeezy bottles and pipe stars on to hot dogs and open burgers or sandwiches. If you have a star cutter, you can make cheesy star biscuits, too. Find a recipe for cheese straws or biscuits in a cookery book, and use orange cheese to make your stars colourful. Stars stamped out of yellow peppers look very effective too – thread them on to cocktail sticks (mind the points – they're sharp!) with mini frankfurters and cubes of cheese. Stick your finished cocktail sticks in an upside-down grapefruit half to display them.

Star cutters are also great for stamping out tiny sandwiches or jelly stars. Make some jelly with half the usual amount of liquid and pour it into a shallow tray to set in the fridge before stamping out the stars. Serve them with your favourite ice cream and sprinkles or chocolate stars to make a starry sundae.

A star birthday cake is easy to make out of a circular sponge. Make a template of the right size, drawing round the cake tin as your guide. Then, when the cake is baked and has cooled down, lay the template on top and cut around it. Cover the cake with icing and decorate it with silver balls and tiny sweets.

Star light, star bright

You can make brilliant star lanterns out of jam jars and greaseproof, tracing or tissue paper. Use a double layer of tissue paper as it's so thin. You'll also need some little candle night lights. First, cut a collar of paper long enough to fit around the jam jar and a few centimetres taller than the jar (lay the jar on the paper and use it as a guide). Cut the top into a zigzag pattern,

 and decorate the paper with stick-on stars. Then wrap it around the jar, and fasten at the back with Sellotape.

Ask an adult to help you light a night-light and lower it into the jar with a spoon (this can be tricky). A row of these lanterns in different colours looks fantastic, especially arranged along a windowsill.

You can also make paper bag lanterns – but you must keep them outside in the garden or on your doorstep, because of the fire risk. Find some strong brown paper bags (DIY stores often have them). Spray them gold if you like, and you can also cut star shapes in the sides. Then fill them about a third full of sand and put a candle in the middle, stuck into the sand. When an adult lights the candle, the whole bag will start to glow. Make sure you don't cut the shapes too far down the bag, or the sand will spill out.

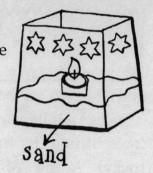

sand

Last but not least – if you're having a sleepover, remember to look out for the first star in the sky and say this traditional rhyme before you make a wish. It's bound to come true!

Star light, star bright,
First star I see tonight,
I wish I may, I wish I might,
Have the wish I wish tonight.

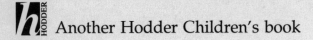
Another Hodder Children's book

JESS'S DISCO DISASTER
Party Girls 2

Jennie Walters

Jess knows exactly what she wants for
her birthday this year: a disco. Trouble is,
she has to convince her twin brother Matt
that he's going to enjoy the party too –
and that's only the start of her problems?
She still has to sort out the guest list, the
music and, most important of all, her
outfit. Are Jess's disco diva dreams going
to end in disaster?

h HODDER Another Hodder Children's book

SUNNY'S DREAM TEAM
Party Girls 3

Jennie Walters

Sunny may be clever, but ordinary girls like her don't win national magazine competitions. At least, that's what her friends think – until Sunny proves them wrong! No she's won a dream prize for herself and the gang; a makeover and a photo shoot with the magazine, supper in a swanky café and an overnight stay in a luxury hotel! But she can only take *four* friends with her . . . who on earth is she going to leave out?

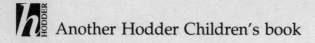
Another Hodder Children's book

MICHELLE'S BIG BREAK
Party Girls 4

Jennie Walters

Summer's here, and Michelle and her
friends are off to a holiday village for a
long weekend of non-stop fun. It's going
to be great: partying, cycling, swimming
and – singing? Yep, singing, Michelle's
discovered there's a talent contest coming
up, and she's determined to take her
favourite position – centre stage!

h HODDER Another Hodder Children's book

NIKKI'S TREASURE TRAIL
Party Girls 5

Jennie Walters

Nikki's life is about to change in a big
way. With her family planning to leave
the neighbourhood, she has no idea what
the future holds – and just when she
needs her friends most, they seem to be
playing it cool. If ever she felt like a party
to cheer her up, it's now. But can the
others be bothered to throw one for her?
It doesn't look like it . . .

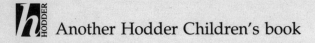

Another Hodder Children's book

LAUREN'S SPOOKY SLEEPOVER
Party Girls 6

Jennie Walters

Lauren's planned a mega Hallowe'en party, with all the trimmings; ghostly games, pumpkin lanterns, freaky costumes, the lot! When the trick-or-treating finishes, her best friends stay on for a sleepover – and that's when things start getting *really* scary! This is definitely *not* the best night to find yourself all alone in the cold and dark . . .

PARTY GIRLS
Jennie Walters

All Hodder & Stoughton books are available at your local bookshop or newsagent, or can be ordered direct from the publisher. Just tick the titles you want and fill in the form below. Prices and availability subject to change without notice.

Hodder & Stoughton Books, Cash Sales Department, Bookpoint, 39 Milton Park, Abingdon, OXON, OX14 4TD, UK. E-mail address: orders@bookprint.co.uk. If you have a credit card you may order by telephone – (01235) 400414.

Please enclose a cheque or postal order made payable to Bookpoint Ltd to the value of the cover price and allow the following for postage and packing:
UK & BFPO: £1.00 for the first book, 50p for the second book and 30p for each additional book ordered up to a maximum charge of £3.00.
OVERSEAS & EIRE: £2.00 for the first book, £1.00 for the second book and 50p for each additional book.

Name ....

Address ....

....

....

If you would prefer to pay by credit card, please complete:
Please debit my Visa / Access / Diner's Club / American Express (delete as applicable) card no:

Signature ....

Expiry Date ....

If you would NOT like to receive further information on our products please tick the box. ☐